This book belongs to:

_____

A day with The Queen

By Diana Del-Negro

To my daughters Laura and Alice with love

-*Hello! My name is Monty.*

Welcome to London, capital of the United Kingdom and home to the British royal family.

Would you like to meet The Queen?

Then come along with me! Her Majesty is expecting you.

The Queen has several homes in different parts of the country, but she spends most of her time at Buckingham Palace, which is her home and office in London.

Do you see that flag on a mast above the Palace? It is called the Royal Standard, and it means that the Queen is at home today. When she's not in the Palace, the Union flag flies instead.

Oh! The Queen's guards are marching in front of us. Let's go through carefully...

The Queen's guards protect the Palace and everybody inside.

-Hello Mr Guard!

-Hello Monty. I see that you have brought guests today.

-Yes. Can we please come in?

-Of course you may. Welcome!

We can see some portraits of The Queen's ancestors here. Did you know that The Queen is a descendant of Queen Victoria and King Edward VII?

QUEEN VICTORIA

KING EDWARD VII

King George V was her grandfather and King George VI, who reigned
during World War II, was her dear father.

KING GEORGE V

KING GEORGE VI

Queen Elizabeth II is not only Queen of the United Kingdom, but she is also the Head of State of fifteen other countries around the world, including Canada, Australia, New Zealand, Jamaica, and several other countries in the Caribbean and Pacific.

These countries are all members of The Commonwealth, which is an association that aims to bring peace and prosperity to all its members.

As a result of being Queen in so many places, the portrait of The Queen appears on the bank notes and coins of many different countries. In fact, Her Majesty appears on the coinage of more countries than any other person in the world!

The Queen has been married to Prince Philip, the Duke of Edinburgh, for more than 70 years. They have four children together: Prince Charles, Princess Anne, Prince Andrew and Prince Edward.

As the eldest son, Prince Charles is the heir to the throne, followed by his son Prince William and his grandson Prince George.

Did you know that The Queen is the longest-reigning monarch in British history? She's been ruling for more than 60 years.

Are you ready to meet Her Majesty? I think she's expecting us…

-Hello Monty! I see you have brought special guests.

  Would you like to spend the day with me?

-Yes, we would!

-Very well. First, we will have a meeting with the Prime Minister.

There have been 13 Prime Ministers so far during Queen Elizabeth II's reign.

Sir Winston Churchill was the first Prime Minister to serve under Her Majesty.

The Queen has a meeting with the Prime Minister every week to discuss government matters.

Although she cannot make laws and stays out of public political debates, she can still encourage, advise and warn her ministers.

The meetings are private and no one knows exactly what they talk about, but we can imagine that The Queen discusses how the country is being managed, what new laws are being prepared and how the Prime Minister plans to solve certain problems.

Did you know that The Queen must sign off on all new laws produced by the government? This approval of a new law is called Royal Assent.

The Queen receives a very important red box every day with documents from her government that she must read and sign.

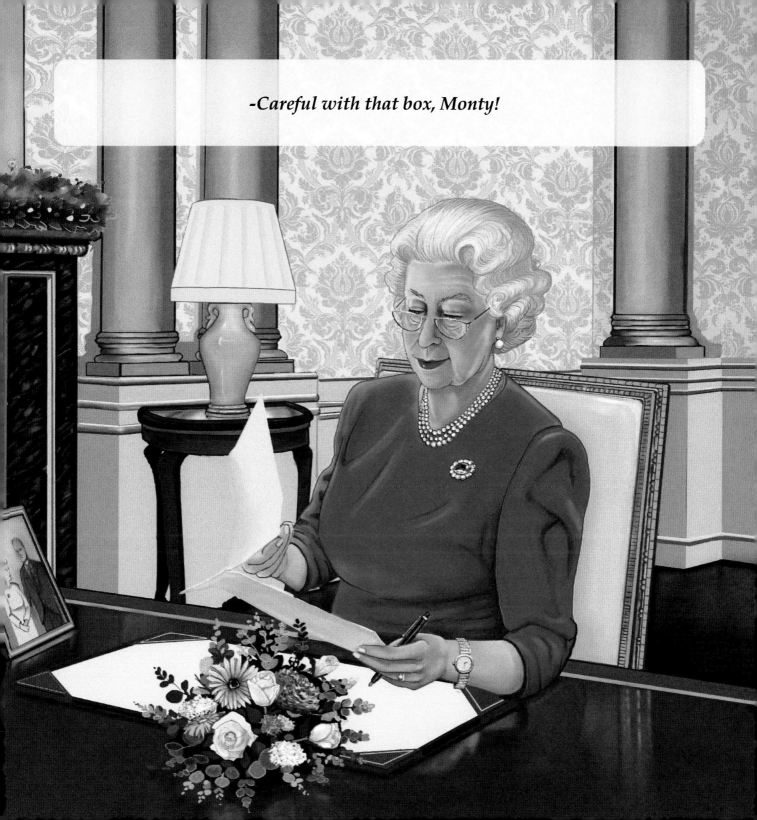

-I am sorry to interrupt, dear... But should we be getting ready to leave?

-Indeed. I have just finished reading and signing this new law.

-Come along Monty, we are going to a party.

-A party? Oh, I just love parties!

The royal family attend many parties, receptions and events in support of charities, the government and the country. However, I am almost never invited...

-Where is the party? I can't wait to get there!

- Calm down, Monty, you can fall out the window! You'll find out where we're going very soon.

-Welcome to Prince George's party!

-Hello Lupo, my dear friend! What a wonderful surprise!

-Hello, Granny!

-Hello, George. Happy birthday!

We have brought a very special gift for you, but you will have to promise to take very good care of it.

-I promise!

-A pony! Thank you!

-You're welcome, George. We hope you enjoy riding her.

- Yes! We will be the best of friends!

It's time to say goodbye for now. I hope you've enjoyed this day with Her Majesty and her beautiful family.

I hope to see you again soon!

Made in the USA
Middletown, DE
19 June 2020